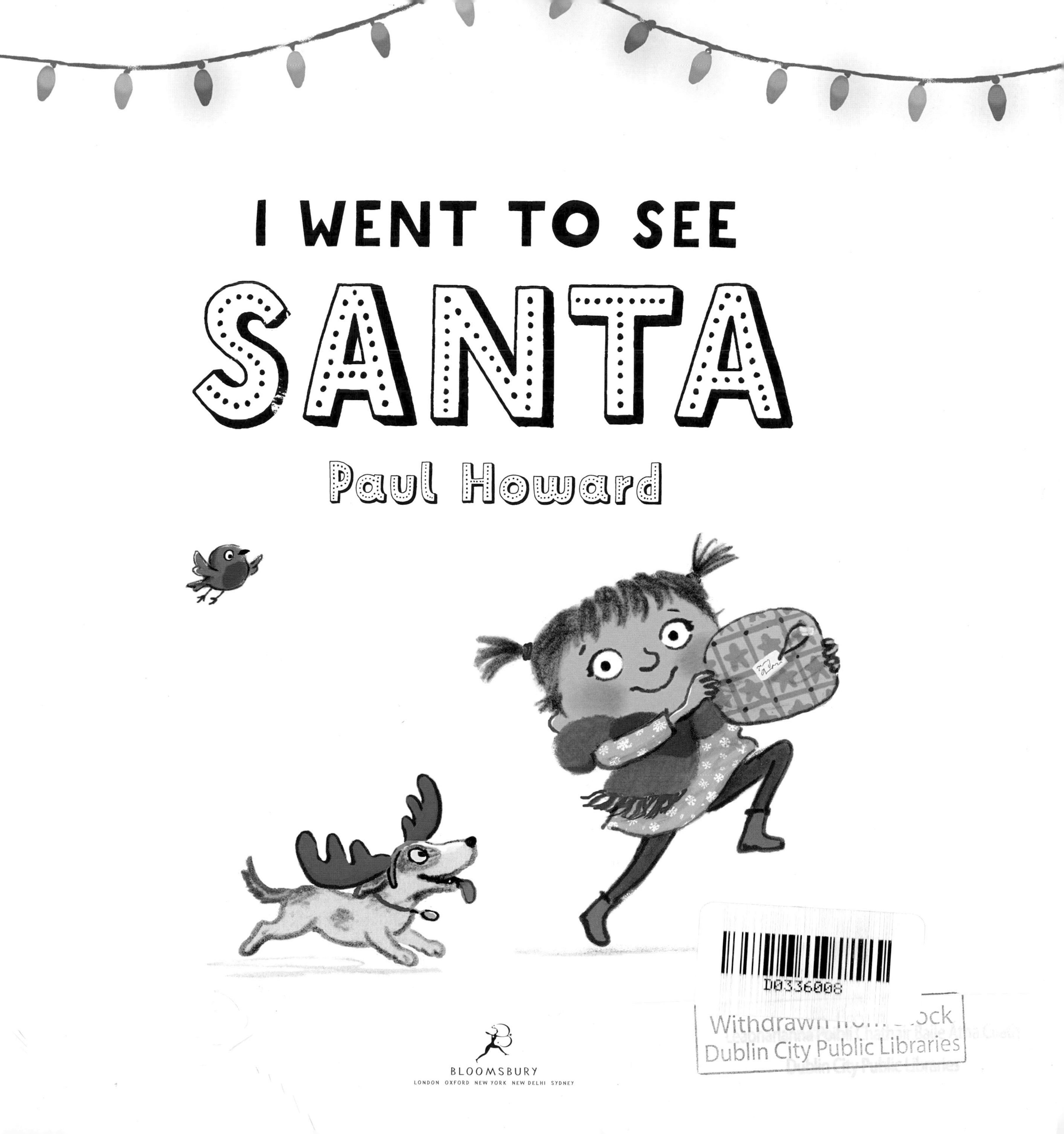

I WENT TO SEE SANTA

Paul Howard

BLOOMSBURY
LONDON OXFORD NEW YORK NEW DELHI SYDNEY

For my mum and dad

Bloomsbury Publishing, London, Oxford, New York, New Delhi and Sydney

First published in Great Britain in 2017 by Bloomsbury Publishing Plc
50 Bedford Square, London, WC1B 3DP

www.bloomsbury.com

BLOOMSBURY is a registered trademark of Bloomsbury Publishing Plc

A CIP catalogue record for this book is available from the British Library

ISBN 978 1 4088 4471 7 (HB)
ISBN 978 1 4088 4472 4 (PB)
ISBN 978 1 4088 4473 1 (eBook)

All papers used by Bloomsbury Publishing are natural, recyclable products
made from wood grown in well-managed forests.
The manufacturing processes conform to the environmental regulations of the country of origin

Printed in China by Leo Paper Products, Heshan, Guangdong

1 3 5 7 9 10 8 6 4 2

I went to see **Santa** and I got . . .

a pair of
Christmas
glasses.

Well . . .

I went to see

Santa

and I got a pair

of Christmas glasses

and . . .

an AMAZING
MAGIC
SET.

I went to see

Santa

and I got a pair

of Christmas glasses,

an AMAZING MAGIC SET

and...

a friendly
reindeer!

Well I went to see

SANTA

and I got a pair of

Christmas glasses,

an AMAZING

MAGIC SET,

a *friendly reindeer*

and...

some

pirate treasure.

I went to see
SANTA
and I got a pair of
Christmas glasses,
an AMAZING MAGIC SET,
a friendy reindeer, some
pirate treasure and . . .

seven skating

PENGUINS!

Well I went to see SANTA and I got
a pair of Christmas glasses,
an AMAZING MAGIC SET,
a friendly reindeer,
some pirate treasure,
seven skating
PENGUINS
and...

a *SUPER BEAR*.

I went to see SANTA
and I got a pair of
Christmas glasses, an
AMAZING MAGIC SET, a friendly
reindeer, some pirate treasure,
seven skating PENGUINS,
a *SUPER BEAR* and...

a ***SPACE ROCKET!***

Well I went to see SANTA
and I got a pair of
Christmas glasses,
an AMAZING MAGIC SET,
a friendly reindeer,
some pirate treasure,
seven skating PENGUINS,
a *SUPER BEAR*,
a ***SPACE ROCKET*** and . . .

a band of
Merry Christmas
Elves.

I went to see SANTA
and I got a pair of Christmas
glasses, an AMAZING MAGIC SET,
a friendly reindeer, some pirate
treasure, seven skating PENGUINS,
a *SUPER BEAR*, a ***SPACE
ROCKET***, a band of
Merry Christmas
Elves and...

a gingerbread
TREE.

I went to see SANTA and I got
a pair of Christmas glasses,
an AMAZING MAGIC SET, a friendly reindeer,
some pirate treasure,
seven skating PENGUINS,
a *SUPER BEAR*, a ***SPACE ROCKET***,
a band of Merry Christmas Elves,
a gingerbread TREE
and...

lots of

SNOWBALLS.

I went to see SANTA
and I got a pair of Christmas glasses,
an
AMAZING
MAGIC
SET,
a friendly
reindeer,
some
pirate treasure,

seven skating
PENGUINS,
a SUPER BEAR,
a SPACE ROCKET,
a band of Merry
Christmas Elves,
a gingerbread
TREE and...
lots of
SNOWBALLS!
Hee-hee-hee!

a pair of
Christmas glasses,
an AMAZING
MAGIC SET,
a
friendly
reindeer,
some
pirate treasure,
seven skating
PENGUINS,
Oh, ha-ha, very funny!
Well I win anyway
because YOU forgot something...

a SUPER BEAR,
a SPACE ROCKET,
a band of Merry Christmas Elves,
a gingerbread TREE and...
lots of SNOWBALLS.
Hmm, let me see...

OH NO
I DIDN'T!

OH YES

YOU DID!

You forgot...

IT'S CHR

ISTMAS!

HO! HO! HO!

Merry Christmas,
everyone!